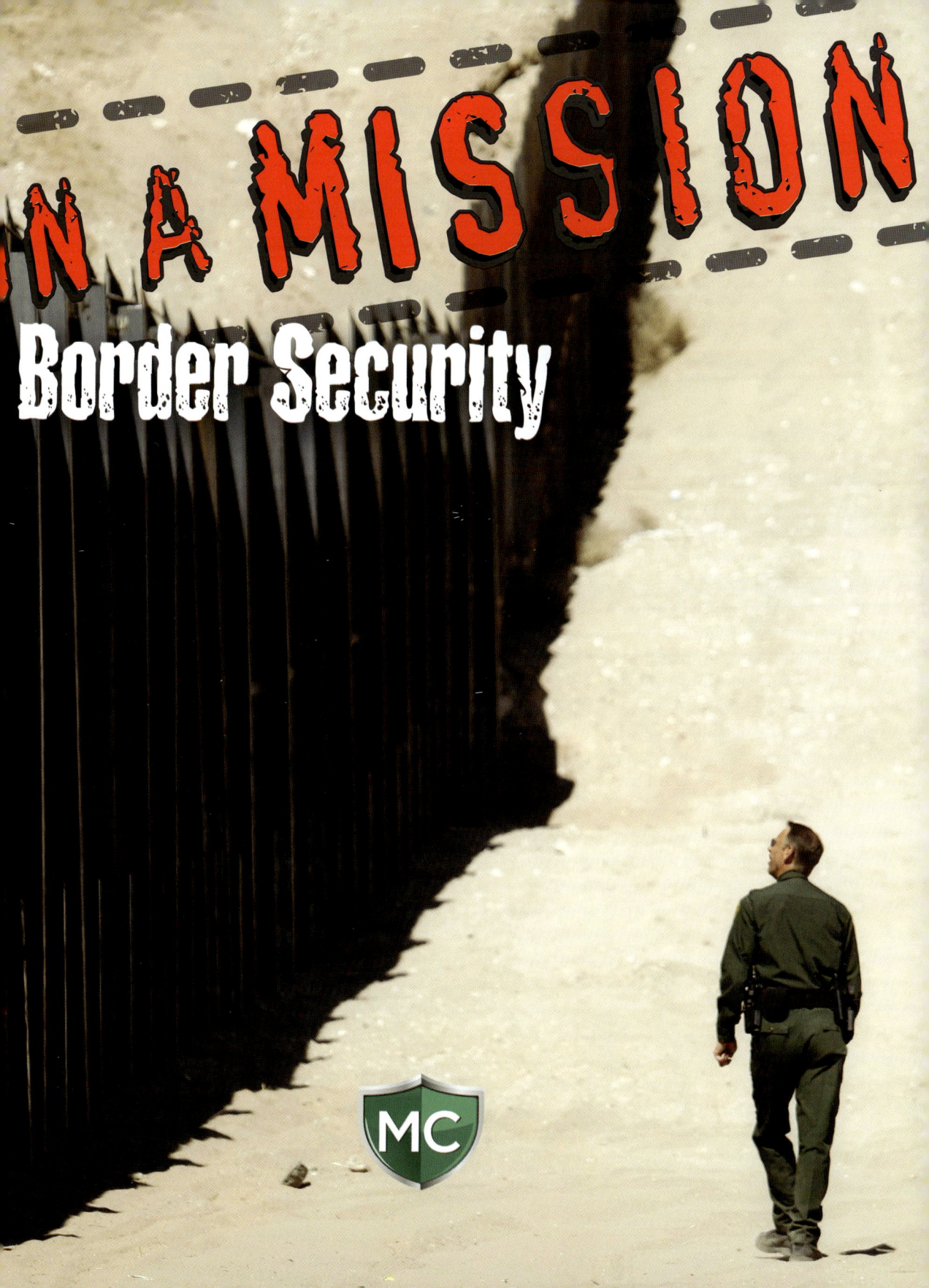

ON A MISSION

Bomb Squad Technician

Border Security

Dogs on Patrol

FBI Agent

Fighter Pilot

Firefighter

Paramedic

Search and Rescue Team

Secret Service Agent

Special Forces

SWAT Team

Undercover Police Officer

ON A MISSION
Border Security

By John Perritano

SOMERSET CO. LIBRARY
BRIDGEWATER, N.J. 08807

Mason Crest
450 Parkway Drive, Suite D
Broomall, PA 19008
www.masoncrest.com

© 2016 by Mason Crest, an imprint of National Highlights, Inc.
All rights reserved. No part of this publication may be reproduced or transmitted in any form or by any means, electronic or mechanical, including photocopying, recording, taping, or any information storage and retrieval system, without permission from the publisher.

Printed and bound in the United States of America.

Series ISBN: 978-1-4222-3391-7
Hardback ISBN: 978-1-4222-3393-1
EBook ISBN: 978-1-4222-8502-2

First printing
1 3 5 7 9 8 6 4 2

Produced by Shoreline Publishing Group LLC

Santa Barbara, California
Editorial Director: James Buckley Jr.
Designer: Bill Madrid
Production: Sandy Gordon
www.shorelinepublishing.com

Cover image: Newscom/MCT/Fort Worth Star-Telegram/Tom Pennington

Library of Congress Cataloging-in-Publication Data

Perritano, John.
    Border security / by John Perritano.
        pages cm. -- (On a mission!)
    Includes index.
ISBN 978-1-4222-3393-1 (hardback) -- ISBN 978-1-4222-3391-7 (series) -- ISBN 978-1-4222-8502-2 (ebook) 1. Border security--United States--Juvenile literature. 2. Border patrols--United States--Juvenile literature. 3. U.S. Border Patrol--Juvenile literature. 4. National security--United States--Juvenile literature. I. Title.
JV6483.P47 2016
363.28'502373--dc23

                              2015004838

Contents

Emergency!	6
Mission Prep	12
Training Mind and Body	20
Tools and Technology	30
Mission Accomplished!	40
Find Out More	46
Series Glossary	47
Index/About the Author	48

Key Icons to Look For

Words to Understand: These words with their easy-to-understand definitions will increase the reader's understanding of the text, while building vocabulary skills.

Sidebars: This boxed material within the main text allows readers to build knowledge, gain insights, explore possibilities, and broaden their perspectives by weaving together additional information to provide realistic and holistic perspectives.

Research Projects: Readers are pointed toward areas of further inquiry connected to each chapter. Suggestions are provided for projects that encourage deeper research and analysis.

Text-Dependent Questions: These questions send the reader back to the text for more careful attention to the evidence presented here.

Series Glossary of Key Terms: This back-of-the-book glossary contains terminology used throughout this series. Words found here increase the reader's ability to read and comprehend higher-level books and articles in this field.

Emergency!

A ferry crossing like this one posed a unique challenge for a U.S. Border Patrol agent.

A few more minutes.

That's all Ahmed Ressam needs.

His is the last car in line.

Be calm. Be smart. Then you're good to go. Home free, as the Americans say.

It's 5:30 P.M. on December 14, 1999, and the last ferry of the day has just docked. Ressam had a lot of time to think during the two-hour crossing. He had driven aboard the ferry at Victoria, a town just south of Vancouver, in the Canadian province of British Columbia. The ride across the Strait of Juan de Fuca was uneventful. Now he was here in Port Angeles, Washington, waiting to cross into the United States.

Like all the passengers getting off the ferry, Ressam expects to answer a few questions from U.S. Border Patrol inspectors. Afterwards, he'll be on his way.

You can do it. Stay cool. Stay calm. It'll be okay.

Ressam waits in his rental car—the last car in Lane 2, the center lane—Diane Dean's lane.

Words to Understand
asylum protection by a government to someone who has fled another country
emblazoned decorated with a symbol, writing, or picture
passport official government document that allows a person to travel from country to country
warrant official document that allows the police to do something such as arrest a person

Inspection

Most of the inspections at the Port Angeles crossing take place outdoors where the wind and the salt air skip off the water. The inspectors stand next to gray tables bolted together from scrap lumber. They question those coming off the ferry. *What's your name? Where are you coming from? Why are you going? How long will you stay?* If an inspector needs to make a phone call or check the computer, they walk to a ramshackle trailer, where wayward sparrows and seagulls nest in the rafters. The inspectors feed the birds.

Border security agents around the world make sure that the people coming into their countries are who they say they are.

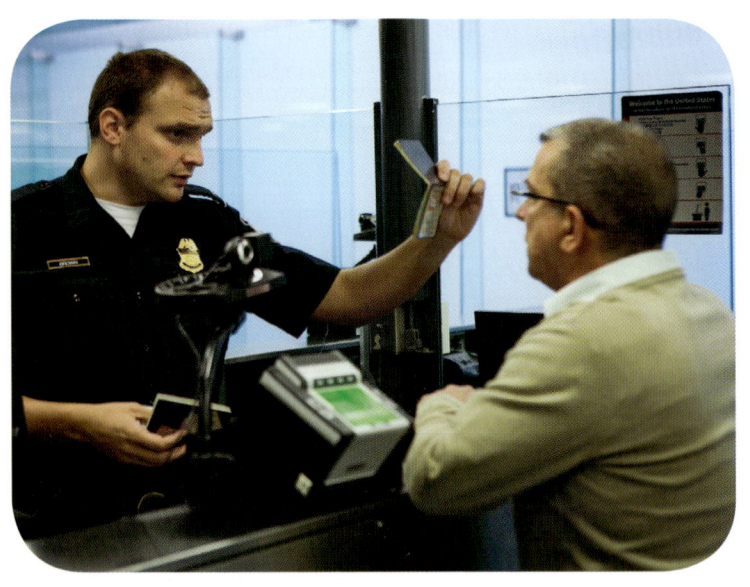

One by one, the border agents ask their questions. One by one, they wave travelers through. One by one, the cars move up Lane 2.

The longer Ressam waits, the more nervous he becomes. He carries a Canadian **passport** and a Costco card, each **emblazoned** with the fake name, Benni Antoine Noris.

Stay calm. You'll be fine.

He starts to sweat.

They'll never find the explosives. I've hidden them well.

Terrorist in Waiting

Born in 1967 in a poor town in Algeria, a country in North Africa, Ressam moved to Canada in 1994 using a fake French passport in which he crudely glued his photo. The passport was easy for Canadian customs officials to spot. Suspecting the document to be fake, Canadian immigration officials peppered Ressam with questions.

Ressam eventually admitted the passport wasn't real and asked for political **asylum**. He claimed that he had been tortured in Algeria. To go back would mean his death. The Canadians allowed Ressam to stay in their country. Soon, however, using fake documents, he created a new identity and vanished like a puff of smoke. He was now Benni Antoine Noris, and no one in Canada was the wiser.

For five years, Ressam lived in Canada as Noris. However, Ressam wanted to be a terrorist, too. In 1998, he flew from Montreal to Afghanistan to train in one of Osama bin Laden's terrorist camps. He returned to Canada in 1999, armed with the knowledge of how to make a bomb.

By August, Ressam had hatched a plan to bomb the Los Angeles International Airport. By the fall, he had built the timing devices needed to set off the explosives. By mid-November, Ressam was in Vancouver gathering all the other materials to complete the plan. He and an associate later rented a motel room and set up a bomb-making factory.

The plan was to rent a car, cross the border with the explosives, drive to Los Angeles, and plant the bombs.

Crossing Over

The rental car inches closer up Lane 2. Inspector Diane Dean cheerfully goes about her job.

"When I'm working a car, I'm always glancing at the next one behind," Dean later told the *Seattle Times*. "If it looks like grandma and grandpa…it probably is. You're going to ask different questions depending on whether they have U.S. or Canadian plates. You eyeball that person and see if what they look like matches with who they say they are."

To Dean, everyone seems like "regular, normal people."

Everyone, that is, except the man with a fake name in a car he doesn't own that is crammed with explosives.

Later, in the final chapter "Mission Accomplished," find out how this potentially deadly enemy was prevented from entering the United States. First, read more about how border security experts do their work.

Anyone driving into the United States can be stopped and questioned. Agents check that they have the right papers and identification.

Chapter 1

A link to the past: Some of today's Border Patrol agents still ride horseback, as the first agents did more than a century ago.

Mission Prep

The United States shares 6,000 miles (9,656 km) of land border with Canada and Mexico. In addition, there are more than 2,000 miles (3,218 km) of coastal waters surrounding Florida and the territory of Puerto Rico.

Who protects such a vast area? Who makes sure that weapons, criminals, terrorists, and others don't enter the country illegally? That job falls to the 21,000 Border Patrol agents of U.S. Customs and Border Protection (CBP)—also known as the U.S. Border Patrol. The CBP is the largest police force in the United States.

Storied History

The U.S. Border Patrol has a long and **storied** history. Although it was first formed in 1924, its origins date back to 1904, when inspectors

Words to Understand

cantinas Spanish word for bars or saloons
consumption to eat or drink
gangsters members of a criminal gang
importation to bring something into one country from another country
smugglers people who carries goods illegally into a country
storied celebrated

from the U.S. Immigration Service patrolled the Canadian and Mexican borders on horseback.

Many of those working for the patrol in the 1920s were former Texas Rangers, local sheriffs, and deputies. Each had to provide his own horse and saddle, although the government furnished food for the horses. The government also gave the inspectors a badge and a gun.

The government paid the inspectors $1,680 a year (still only about $20,000 in today's dollars). At the time, only a few people took the job. As a result, the army was often called to patrol the border. In the early 1920s, the need to secure the borders increased greatly after the Eighteenth Amendment to the U.S. Constitution was passed. That amendment outlawed the **importation**, transportation, and **consumption** of alcohol. Because of the law, known as Prohibition, **smugglers** and **gangsters** did a

Modern moves: Vehicles such as this ATV are able to reach just about anywhere in search of trouble at a border.

brisk business illegally moving alcohol across the border, especially from Canada. Although they still used horses, many agents began patrolling in motorized vehicles.

Since then, the Border Patrol has grown rapidly. It soon took over the security work done at airports, train stations, and other ports of entry into the United States. A series of laws gave the Border Patrol the power to make sure that people were coming into the country with the proper documents and not bringing in illegal goods.

The terrorist attacks on New York City and Washington, D.C., on September 11, 2001, led to big changes in how America operates its borders. Congress rearranged the entire national security system in the wake of the attacks. As of 2003, the CBP became part of the new U.S. Department of Homeland Security. Among the CBP's many priorities, agents are on the lookout for terrorists crossing the border. Still, an important part of CBP's mission remains to make sure people and goods can travel legally and safely between countries.

Not only do border agents look for people, weapons, drugs, and other outlawed items, but they also keep an eye out for dangerous animals, plants, insects, and other pests that can harm the environment.

On Duty at Ports of Entry

On a map, the borders of the United States don't seem to be that dangerous. However, those are only lines on a map. The borders include remote deserts, islands, canyons, inhospitable mountains, and treacherous waterways.

The difficult terrain makes security a challenge. Many people are creative when smuggling people, weapons, drugs, and other things across the border. They dig tunnels and hide in container ships. One man once sewed himself into the seat of a car hoping to elude border agents.

Although the borders are long, much of an agent's work is centered on ports of entry, specific locations where people and goods can pass into the country. In New York state, one port is near the sleepy town of Rouses Point, while in California it might be the very busy border crossing just south of San Diego. As of 2014, there were 328 ports of entry into the United States.

Border patrol agents must possess many skills. Before they put on a badge or shoulder a gun, agents have to pass a fitness test and an extensive examination. They must also complete 58 days of training at the U.S. Border Patrol Academy in Artesia, New Mexico.

At the academy, agents learn about the country's immigration and public health laws. They have to go through an intensive physical training course and learn how to be good marksmen. For those wanting to work at the Mexican border, being fluent in Spanish helps. Those who don't speak Spanish will spend an additional 40 days learning the language.

Different Jobs

The U.S. Border Patrol has a variety of specialties, including:

- **Agriculture Specialist:** Agents use scientific skills to inspect food and animals coming into the country.

- **Air Interdiction Agent:** Agents use helicopters and airplanes to patrol the border.

- **Marine Interdiction Agent:** Agents patrol the coast of the country, often on the water in boats or ships.

- **CBP Officer:** Agents on duty at border crossings inspect visitors, check paperwork, and prevent terrorists and their weapons from entering the country.

- **Import Specialist:** Agents decide which products can enter the country legally. They also play a key role in criminal investigations relating to smuggling.

On the Job

In 2013, Border Patrol agents processed 362 million pedestrians and vehicles, and more than 102 million passengers flying into the United States. However, many have tried to pull one over them by bringing things into the country that they shouldn't. For example, in 2013, agents:

- seized 2.8 million pounds of illegal drugs;
- apprehended 420,789 illegal aliens;
- stopped 1,603,944 plants and animals from entering the ports.

More Than Meets the Eye

Working as a Border Patrol agent means a lot more than checking passengers who come to the United States for business or on vacation. Jesus Carrillo, who worked as an undercover agent on the Mexican border, knows firsthand how dangerous the job can be.

Born in Mexico, Carrillo came to the United States, became a citizen, and volunteered for service in the U.S. Army during the Vietnam War (1964–1975). He joined the U.S. Border Patrol in 1971.

At the time, the American Southwest was ground zero for groups of people who smuggled immigrants and illegal drugs from Mexico to the U.S. Carrillo went to work each morning not in the green uniform of the Border Patrol, but in civilian clothes. He told a reporter he never "dressed down." Instead, he wore flashy gold jewelry, an expensive cowboy hat, and fancy leather boots, so he could look the part of a drug lord.

Carrillo hung out in local **cantinas** in West Texas and Southern New Mexico for more than a dozen years. Inside these watering holes, he bought illegal drugs and gathered enough evidence to put criminals in jail.

In 1996, members of a Mexican drug gang wanted to kill him, but the Federal Bureau of Investigation (FBI) arrested the would-be hit men near Carrillo's home. Eventually, Carrillo retired, but he's still worried that a drug smuggler will hurt him. "I'm still armed all the time," he says. "But I loved wearing the green uniform."

Text-Dependent Questions

1. Which U.S. government department is now responsible for the CBP?
2. Explain Prohibition and the impact it had on border inspectors.
3. Name and describe three different jobs of the U.S. Border Patrol.

Research Project

Print out or copy a map of the U.S. border with Canada or Mexico. Next, research the ports of entry for one of the borders. Plot the locations of those ports on the map.

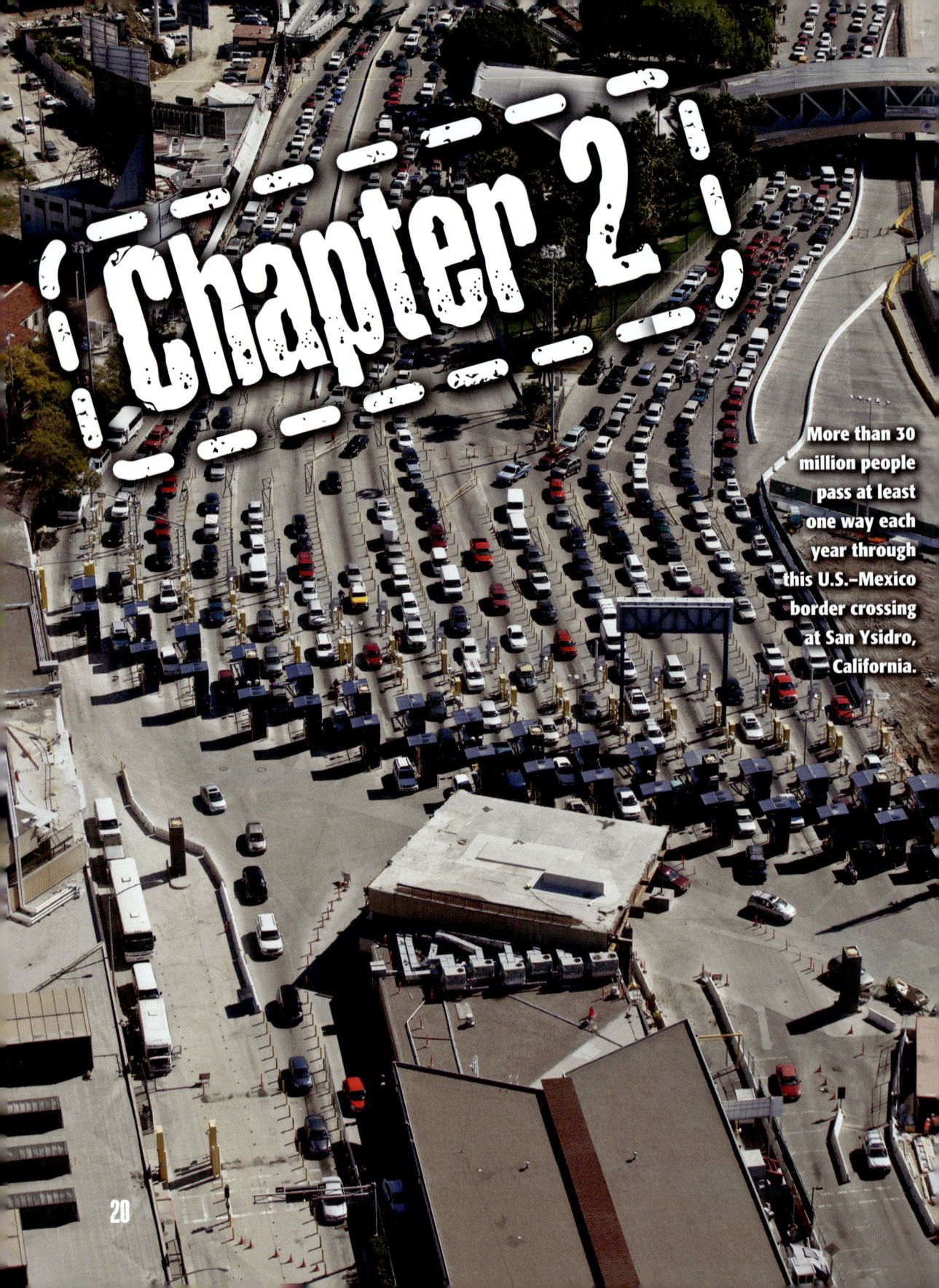

Chapter 2

More than 30 million people pass at least one way each year through this U.S.–Mexico border crossing at San Ysidro, California.

Training Mind and Body

The agents working the San Ysidro port of entry connecting Tijuana, Mexico, and San Diego, California, knew something was up when they spotted the 16-year-old boy. The agent first noticed a problem with the boy's visa, a document that allowed the child to enter the United States as a tourist.

The boy didn't look suspicious. He wore an easy smile and a neatly cropped buzz cut. He had on a white hoodie and blue jeans.

The teenager could have been anyone's son. He was carrying a juice bottle and a large water bottle. Both were filled with an amber-colored liquid.

Words to Understand
alien noncitizen resident of a country
contraband smuggled goods
ethnicity belonging to a racial or cultural group
intellect a person's intelligence
interrogate to question a person as part of an official investigation
visa travel permit issued by a government to a citizen for a specific trip

Was the clear liquid apple juice or some other fruity drink? Something in the agents' minds made them suspicious. Their training told them so. Their experience forced them to look closer.

An officer took one of the bottles and poured a capful of the liquid on the counter. He suspected the liquid might be a drug called *methamphetamine*. If it were that drug, it would instantly evaporate outside the bottle and leave behind crystals.

Nothing. The liquid stayed as it was. It even smelled fruity.

"It's apple juice," the boy said. He then took a swig to show everyone.

Suddenly, the boy grabbed his chest and screamed, "My heart! My heart!"

The boy fell to the floor. The agents called 911. An ambulance arrived and the agents handcuffed the boy to a gurney. It turned out the "apple juice" was 90 percent liquid methamphetamine. The boy was cared for, but was taken into custody for trying to smuggle drugs.

The job of a Border Patrol agent is often difficult. They must be constantly looking for things that are masked as something else. Guided by their experience, their training, and their **intellect**, if a guard thinks something is suspicious, then it probably is.

Tough School

The CBP Border Patrol Academy in Artesia, New Mexico, is in the middle of nowhere, just south of the city of Roswell. Many consider the school one of the toughest police academies in the United States. That's because working the border can be demanding. Before leaving the academy, a recruit has to be able to run a mile-and-a-half in thirteen minutes, complete a "confidence course" in two-and-a-half minutes, and run the 220-yard (201 m) dash in 46 seconds. They also learn how to **interrogate** people,

Future Border Patrol agents have to study the science of agriculture to help prevent dangerous foods or plants from entering the United States.

At the Border Patrol Academy, physical fitness is part of the work. Here, students work out on an obstacle course.

people, how to handle a vehicle during high-speed chases, and how to shoot accurately.

As soon as trainees arrive at the academy, they are given a fake sidearm so they can get used to wearing one every day. "We have to treat it exactly the same, no taking it out of our belt and playing with it. It's always here, just like it'll be in the field," Keven Ekkebus, a Border Patrol trainee, told CBS News.

Although some of the classes at the academy are exciting, the recruits must also learn that standing a post at a lonely border crossing can be boring at times, with only brief moments of excitement.

The training is not easy. Only one recruit out of every thirty becomes an agent, while two out of every ten drop out as soon as they arrive.

Talking the Talk

Speaking the language of the border, whether near Mexico in Texas or near French-speaking Canada in Minnesota, is an important part of the job. Those working the southern border must learn a year's worth of Spanish in five months. Soon after arriving at the academy, the trainees are tested on their language skills. Those who fail the test are put into Spanish classes. Those who already speak Spanish continue with their training.

Uncooperative People

Sometimes people will not answer questions that border agents ask. Agents at checkpoints in the United States can ask people basic questions about their citizenship, who they are, and why they're traveling. However, the agents cannot detain a person or search their vehicle just because that person refuses to answer questions.

Why is that? The Fourth Amendment to the U.S. Constitution protects Americans from "unreasonable searches and seizures." Refusing to answer a question from a Border Patrol agent does not give the agent probable cause, or sufficient reason, to detain or search a vehicle.

Once they are on the job, most agents find themselves questioning all sorts of people. They must learn to determine in a short time whether a person is an **alien**, a legal visitor or citizen of the United States, a terrorist, or a smuggler. They must also look for signs that someone is trying to smuggle **contraband**.

Soliciting information is an art that instructors try to teach the trainees. Agents learn how to talk informally with people and speak in words and phrases that individuals understand.

Applying the Law

Like all police officers, Border Patrol agents must know when a person is violating the law. Agents not only have to learn U.S. immigration laws, but criminal laws as well. They must also learn when to take action because people will do anything to commit a crime.

Such was the case in 2008 when inspectors stopped a 50-year-old Brooklyn, N.Y., man from crossing into Niagara Falls, N.Y., from Canada. The man told border agents that he was returning to the States after buying religious items in Canada. The agents didn't believe the man. They grew more suspicious as they continued to question him.

They were right. The agents found one hundred liquid vials in the man's possession. The man said the containers were filled with "holy water." Agents found, however, that some contained an illegal drug. Agents arrested the man on various charges. The seizure, the port director said, was a good example of "the extraordinary methods" smugglers use.

Agents inspect millions of tons of food each year to make sure that insects and other animals do not invade the United States.

27

What Can CBP Agents Do?

There are many things a Border Patrol agent can and cannot do. For example:

- The CBP can search people arriving at U.S. ports of entry along with their personal effects, including computer and personal electronic devices. They don't have to obtain a warrant for the search.
- They can search noncitizens if they are on a train, airplane or vehicle "within a reasonable distance from any external boundary of the United States."
- CBP agents can pull cars over within one hundred miles of the border if they have a "reasonable suspicion" that the occupants are breaking the law.

What Can't Agents Do?

- Border Patrol agents are not allowed to target, or profile, a person based on their **ethnicity**. Pulling over a car solely based on an occupant's race is a violation of the U.S. Constitution's Fourth Amendment.

- Border Patrol agents are not allowed to search for noncitizens in private homes, although they can search for illegal aliens on "private lands." To enter a home, agents have to obtain a search warrant from a judge.
- Border Patrol agents cannot threaten a person they are questioning or deny him or her their legal rights.

Text-Dependent Questions

1. List three things a Border Patrol agent cannot do.
2. Explain the concept of "probable cause."
3. In which state is the Border Patrol Academy located?

Research Project

Create a list of contraband items that Border Patrol agents must always be on the lookout for.

Research and write a brief report on the Fourth Amendment to the U.S. Constitution. In your report, explain how the amendment might be applied in a criminal investigation.

Chapter 3

Border Patrol agents help out in disasters near the border. Here, an agent uses an ATV to help residents get through floodwaters.

Tools and Technology

Elvis Cooper made his living in a very dangerous way. The 47-year-old from the Bahamas smuggled groups of people into the United States. His career came to an abrupt end on June 5, 2013.

Shortly after midnight, the crew of a U.S. Coast Guard airplane flying over the waters off South Florida near Palm Beach spotted a small boat some 49 miles (79 km) away. The crew of the plane informed Border Patrol agents of the oncoming vessel.

Two Border Patrol boats with armed agents sped to the area. They spotted the boat about 15 miles (24 km) out. As they got closer, the agents ordered the boat's operator to stop. He refused. A high-speed chase began.

As the boats skidded across the dark Atlantic, agents drew their weapons and fired two warning shots. The captain of the rogue boat still refused to stop. The agents then pumped three bullets into the

Words to Understand
capsized overturned on the surface of the water
dirty bombs bombs containing nuclear waste that can be dispersed through the use of explosives
thwarted upset; stopped

Smugglers have fast boats. The Border Patrol's are faster. High-speed craft such as this patrol boat help chase down criminals on oceans and lakes.

boat's engine, killing the motor. On board were Elvis Cooper, its captain, two Brazilian women, and fourteen passengers.

The drama didn't end when the boat came to a halt. When agents boarded the craft, it **capsized**, sending everyone, including one agent, into the ocean. The Border Patrol and Coast Guard rescued everyone.

Back on land, Cooper reportedly told agents that a man named "Shaba" was going to pay him between $2,000 and $10,000 for each person Cooper successfully smuggled into the country.

The two Brazilian women also gave agents leads on the smuggling operation. Agents arrested Cooper and charged him with human trafficking.

The crime would not have been **thwarted** without the fast-moving boats that Border Patrol agents use to guard the nation's coastline. These vessels would have been science fiction in the 1920s, when all border inspectors rode on horseback and carried a small handgun.

Today, it's a different story. From high-speed boats and night-vision goggles, to helicopters, robots and radiation detection devices, the Border Patrol is equipped to handle any situation—and, yes, they still use horses.

Drones

In recent years, the CBP has relied heavily on technology to secure the borders, especially the

Vader

While Darth Vader is the main villain in *Star Wars*, on the border, Vader is a sophisticated airborne radar system used by the Border Patrol. Known technically as the Vehicle Dismount and Exploitation Radar, Vader was developed for use by the U.S. military in Afghanistan to keep an eye on enemy fighters planting roadside bombs.

Mounted on high-flying drones, border agents in Arizona have used the Vader system since 2012. The radar is so sophisticated that it can find and track individuals as the drone flies five miles overhead. The system takes black-and-white images of moving targets and transmits those images to a ground station, where each figure is represented by a moving dot on a map.

southern border with Mexico. The agency's reliance on drones and other high-tech gadgets has allowed the agency, in the words of its director, to "shrink the border." That lets agents focus on areas where smugglers and drug runners are likely to travel.

The idea is to cover 45 percent, or 900 miles (1,448 km) of the Mexican border with packs of roving agents, while monitoring the remaining 55 percent with robotic drones. Drones are another name for a high-flying robotic vehicle called the Unmanned Aerial Vehicle, or UAV.

Drones are large remote-controlled airplanes operated by a pilot sitting hundreds of miles away at a set of controls that look much like a video game. Military drones are equipped with weapons and cameras. Border Patrol drones carry cameras and sensors to find people on the ground.

From March 2013 to November 2014, the CBP launched 10,000 drone flights along the Mexican border. The job of the aerial robots is to look for footprints, broken branches, and tire tracks where they shouldn't be—all telltale signs that someone is trying to enter the country illegally.

If the drone detects a slight disturbance, a team of agents is dispatched to the area. The drones were deployed along the Canadian border in 2015.

Robots

Over the years, drug and weapons smugglers have used a maze of tunnels connecting Nogales, Ariz., and Nogales, Mexico, as a superhighway to ferry people and narcotics. Tracking the criminals was a dirty business. Some tunnels were too dangerous to enter. Cameras could not peer inside, nor could drones

Radiation Portal Monitors

When cars are stopped at a border crossing, radiation monitors screen the vehicles. The devices look for nuclear radiation coming from **dirty bombs**. The fear is that a terrorist will try to smuggle nuclear weapons, including weapons of mass destruction. The CBP also uses the devices at rail crossings, international airports, and international mail facilities.

detect what was happening. Agents even poured concrete inside the tunnels to render them useless. They also installed motion sensors to detect the movements of the smugglers. Every time they shut one tunnel down, though, another tunnel sprung up.

Nothing seemed to work. That all changed when the Border Patrol station in Nogales started

This agent is setting up a tunnel robot that will do the dirty work. Cameras on the robot will help agents see if the tunnel is being used for smuggling.

using robots. Agents now remotely guide the robots through the tunnels. The bots can look up and down, sideways, and back and forth. They can go deep into the tunnels where the air is not safe for a human to breathe.

The robots move quickly through the tunnels, some of which are connected to vacant homes or occupied houses not far from the border. The bots found one large tunnel in 2014 that was lit by lamps. The smugglers hooked up fans to circulate the air.

"If we find a tunnel, we like to send a robot into it to clear the tunnel and identify any threats, contraband, or people with weapons, and let the agent know ahead of time if the tunnel is structurally sound," Border Patrol agent Kevin Hecht said.

Night-Vision Goggles

Many people try to sneak across the border at night, when it's dark and they can hide in the shadows. For Border Patrol officers, the question then becomes: How do you see at night? Night-

Surveillance Towers

Border Patrol agents also rely on surveillance towers equipped with radar and high-tech cameras to keep an eye on the border. The towers along the Canadian and Mexican borders are permanent structures, but the CBP hopes one day to use portable towers equipped with cameras that can see in the dark as well as during the day. The cameras can see a person walking as far away as eight miles. The towers can communicate with agents using a digital relay system. The system allows agents to see what is happening in real time.

vision goggles are the answer. The goggles allow agents to see in the dead of night, sometimes 200 yards (183 m) on a moonless night. The goggles work by taking in the tiny amounts of light from the moon and stars that is reflected from the ground. Special lenses increase that tiny amount of light to allow the viewer to see.

People can also be found by tracking the heat given off by their bodies. Thermal imaging eyewear reads a type of light called infrared, which is let off as heat by objects or people. Using this kind of high-tech lens, Border Patrol officers can spot people even in inky blackness.

Vehicles

Since agents have to transverse many different types of terrain, the vehicles they use have to be able to handle the wear and tear of such rugged conditions. ATVs and pickup trucks can move almost anywhere in any terrain. Other agents drive police interceptor vehicles, motorcycles, small boats, and even snowmobiles.

For really rugged terrain where a motorized car or truck cannot make tracks, Border Patrol agents will ride on horseback, just like in the good old days.

Agents on four legs: Sniffer dogs are used to help find illegal goods.

Text-Dependent Questions

1. Explain how Vader works.
2. Define a dirty bomb.
3. Name two types of special eyewear that the Border Patrol uses in its work.

Research Project

Research how the U.S. military has used drones during the wars in Afghanistan and Iraq.

Chapter 4

An agent never knows if the person sh[e is]
questioning will turn out to be a dan[gerous criminal.]
The agents must always be on gu[ard.]

40

Mission Accomplished!

Earlier in the day before Ahmed Ressam drives into her life at the Port Angeles ferry, Diane Dean is at the firing range shooting targets and practicing takedowns with her fellow agents.

By late afternoon, she's at work. She's in charge of Lane 2, the center lane, Ressam's lane. Working the other lanes and checking foot passengers are Inspectors Mark Johnson, Mike Chapman, and Dan Clem.

Ressam inches his rental car, a dark green Chrysler with British Columbia plates, to the front of Dean's lane. He is extremely nervous.

"Where are you going?" Dean asks, sensing his anxiety.

"Sattal," Ressam stammers.

"Why are you going to Seattle?" she asks.

Ressam tries to say "Visit," but is hard to understand.

"Where do you live?"

Words to Understand
fray battle; conflict
nitroglycerin a highly volatile liquid used in explosives

"Montreal."

That accent. It's French-Canadian, Dean thinks. I get it now. Still, why is he so jittery?

"Who are you going to see in Seattle?"

"No, hotel."

This doesn't make sense.

Ressam fidgets. Dean senses his agitation. His hands are constantly on the move. "When the hands disappear, you get nervous," Dean says later.

Out of the Car

Something is wrong. Dean knows it. She orders Ressam, whose passport says Benni Antoine Noris, out of the car.

Turn the car off. Pop the trunk.

She calls over Johnson, who speaks Spanish.

"*Habla español?*" he asks Ressam, wanting to know if he speaks Spanish.

"*Parlez-vous français?*" Ressam answers. "Do you speak French?"

He gives Johnson his Costco card as a form of identification.

Strange. Very strange.

"So, you like to shop in bulk," Johnson jokes, trying to figure out if Ressam is lying about not speaking English, but the agents are worried.

They lead Ressam over to a table and search the pockets of his trench coat. Other agents take a suitcase from the trunk and remove the spare tire.

The wheel well is crammed with ten green plastic garbage bags. They're filled with white crystals. Agents also find two olive jars full of an amber liquid, two pill bottles, and black boxes.

Drugs, has to be drugs.

The case in these pages involved explosives, but agents also find drugs hidden in many parts of cars. Here, they intercepted wheels filled with bricks of drugs.

Escape

Johnson searches Ressam for weapons. He feels a bulge in his right pocket. Ressam's nervousness gets the best of him. He slips his arms out of his coat and runs. At first Johnson is stunned.

Then Johnson and Chapman give chase. Agent Dean and Inspector Dean Campbell get in their vans. "Watch the trunk!" Dean yells to another agent, standing nearby.

Ressam has a head start and bolts into town. Agents chase Ressam past banks and flower planters, stores and restaurants. Ressam runs into First Street and then dives under a parked pickup truck.

Agent Chapman draws his gun. "Stop! Police! Customs!" he yells.

Ressam doesn't respond. He steps into traffic, bouncing off a moving car as it speeds by, and trying to duck into a parking lot. Then he suddenly spots another agent.

Ressam runs again. On the street, he grabs the door handle of a car stopped at a light. The shocked driver steps on the gas.

Ressam spins. He's knocked off balance.

Chapman tackles him.

Now, Agent Johnson, all 240 pounds (108 kg) of him, enters the **fray**. He kneels on Ressam's shoulders and slaps the cuffs on him.

The chase is over.

The border is secure.

Close Call

Only later do they find out Ressam was carrying explosives. He filled two olive jars with fifty ounces (1.5 l) of *ethylene glycol dinitrate*, an explosive similar to **nitroglycerin**. Luckily, no one picked up the jars. Border inspectors could have set them off by unscrewing the lids. The garbage bags contained 118 pounds (53.5 kg) of fertilizer and sulfate powder. When mixed with other chemicals, these ingredients make a powerful bomb.

The actions of the Border Patrol that day probably saved lives. How many? We'll never know.

After the excitement of that December 14, 1999, Ressam went on trial and then to prison. Dean and her coworkers got medals and went back to work.

"I can't tell you I've led a very exciting life," Diana Dean told a magazine writer for the *Seattle Times* about how her life had been before Ressam drove up Lane 2, the center lane, her lane. "Absolutely not one thing extraordinary. Nothing. Totally boring." Until that day . . . .

Find Out More

Books

Gains, Ann. *Border Patrol Agent and Careers in Border Protection (Homeland Security and Counterterrorism Careers)*. Berkeley Heights, N.J.: Enslow Publications, Inc., 2006.

Hernadez, Kelly Lytle. *Migra!: A History of the U.S. Border Patrol (American Crossroads)*. Berkeley, Calif.: University of California Press, 2010.

Miller, Connie Colewell. *The U.S. Border Patrol: Guarding the Nation (Line of Duty)*. N. Mankato, Minn.: Capstone Press, 2008.

Pacheco, Alex and Krauss, Erich. *On the Line: Inside the U.S. Border Patrol*. Citadel, 2005.

Web Sites

U.S. Customs and Border Protection
www.cbp.gov/

Canada Border Services Agency
www.cbsa-asfc.gc.ca

National Border Patrol Museum
www.borderpatrolmuseum.com/history/history-2

Texas State Historical Association: United States Border Patrol
www.tshaonline.org/handbook/online/articles/ncujh

Series Glossary of Key Terms

apprehending capturing and arresting someone who has committed a crime

assassinate kill somebody, especially a political figure

assessment the act of gathering information and making a decision about a particular topic

contraband material that is illegal to possess

cryptography another word for writing in code

deployed put to use, usually in a military or law-enforcement operation

dispatcher a person who announces emergencies over police radio and helps organize the efforts of first responders

elite among the very best; part of a select group of successful experts

evacuated moved to a safe location, away from danger

federal related to the government of the United States, as opposed to the government of an individual state or city

forensic having to do with crime scene evidence

instinctive based on natural impulse and done without instruction

interrogate to question a person as part of an official investigation

Kevlar an extra-tough fabric used in bulletproof vests

search-and-rescue the work of finding survivors after a disaster occurs, or the team that does this work

stabilize make steady or secure; also, in medicine, make a person safe to transport

surveillance the act of watching another person or a place, usually from a hidden location

trauma any physical injury to the body, usually involving bleeding

visa travel permit issued by a government to a citizen for a specific trip

warrant official document that allows the police to do something, such as arrest a person

Index

Algeria 9
California 17, 21
Canada 8, 9, 10, 13, 15, 25
Carrillo, Jesus 18, 19
Cooper, Elvis 31, 32, 33
Dean, Diane 10, 11, 41, 42
dogs 39
drones 34, 35
duties 28
Florida 31
Fourteenth Amendment 14
Fourth Amendment 26, 29
Mexico 13, 18, 21, 25, 34, 35
New Mexico 17, 19
New York 15, 25, 27
Port Angeles, Washington 7, 8
Prohibition 14
radiation portal monitors 35
Ressam, Ahmed 7, 8, 9, 10, 41, 42, 43, 44
robots 35, 36, 37
Texas Rangers 14
U.S. Border Patrol Academy 17, 23, 24, 25
U.S. Coast Guard 31, 32
U.S. Department of Homeland Security 15
Vader 34

Photo Credits

All photos courtesy Customs and Border Patrol—photographers names noted where known: James Tourtelotte 8, 23, 24, 27; Donna Burton 12, 14; Josh Denmark: 11, 20, 36, 40.

Dreamstime.com/Leo Bruce Hempell: 6.

About the Author

John Perritano is an award-winning journalist, writer, and editor from Southbury, Connecticut, who has written numerous articles and books on a variety of subjects, including science, sports, history, and culture for such publishers as National Geographic, Scholastic, and Time/Life. His articles have appeared on Discovery.com, Popular Mechanics.com, and other magazines and Web sites. He holds a master's degree in American History from Western Connecticut State University.

J 363.285 PER
Perritano, John.
Border security

NOV 2 0 2015